To Oliver

For being good.
MERRY CHRISTMAS!

From

It was a crisp Christmas Eve
and Santa and his reindeers
were busy delivering presents to
all the good boys and girls.

Santa's sleigh zoomed over houses, twisting
and turning silently through the snowy night sky.
Santa squeezed down and up and up and down
chimneys, carefully and quietly delivering
lots of presents.

4

All was going to plan until he reached the second to last house on his list.

Suddenly, Santa realised one of the presents was missing!

The reindeer looked in Santa's sack, they searched everywhere but the present was nowhere to be found! "Oh no!" exclaimed Santa. "It must have fallen off the sleigh!"

Santa wondered what to do.
He had no time to look for the present
but he didn't want to disappoint anyone
on his Christmas list.

Then
Santa had a
FANTASTIC
idea!

He looked at his delivery map to see where they were.
Then he checked his list to see who had been naughty or nice.

Oliver's House

At the very top of the list was Oliver.
So Santa and Blitzen (the smallest of all the reindeer) squeezed down the chimney...

7

his

into

quietly

crept

...and

bedroom.

Oliver yawned,
stretched and rubbed
his eyes. He thought he
was still **dreaming** until Blitzen licked his
face with his long, wet, pink tongue - YUCK!

8

"I need your help!" boomed Santa. He explained that a present had fallen off the sleigh and Santa wanted Oliver to go with Blitzen to find it.

Oliver of course was VERY happy to help.

9

It was cold and snowy outside so Oliver
put on his warmest hat
and favourite
stripy scarf.

Oliver
and Blitzen
looked through
Santa's telescope.

They looked down past the
houses and through the trees,
trying to find the lost present.

Suddenly they spotted it,
sitting on top of a pile of snow
at the bottom of a big hill.

He jumped on Blitzen's back and gave him
a friendly pat and little tickle
behind his fluffy ears.
Then with a gentle nudge they flew
high into the starry night sky.

Up and up they soared

and higher

higher

until Blitzen did a
loop the loop,
a flip and a flop
and landed with a bop
next to the pile of snow...

but the present had gone!

Oliver and Blitzen looked around but couldn't see the present anywhere!

All of a sudden Blitzen's wet nose began to twitch and itch and wibble and wobble. What had he found?

Oliver saw a bright orange carrot sticking out of the snow. "Who likes carrots?" he wondered. Perhaps this was a clue to where the present had gone.

Then they saw a tiny white and grey bunny rabbit.

"Hello Mrs Rabbit, we're **looking** for a missing gift which fell from Santa's sleigh. Have you seen **anything?**"

The bunny **twitched** her nose, rubbed her ears and **pointed** a fluffy white paw at a line of acorns.

14

"Who likes acorns?"
wondered **Oliver**.

Then looking down they noticed a
bouncy red squirrel staring back at them.
They followed him, picking up the **acorns** one by one,
not knowing who or what would be at the end of the trail.

As they picked up the final acorn, they noticed a nose-less, button-less, very sad snowman right in front of them.

His carrot nose had fallen off and his acorn buttons had been lost but there, poking out from under his black hat, was a shiny Christmas present!

16

Hurray, they had found the present...
but why did the snowman have it?

The sad snowman explained that
every year he felt forgotten as
he never received a present.
When he found this one he was so
happy. However, now he knew
it belonged to someone
else, he wanted to
give it back.

Feeling sorry for the snowman,
Oliver decided to help.
He placed the half-eaten **carrot**
on the snowman's face for his nose
and the **acorn** buttons on his body –
but the snowman still looked sad.

Then **Oliver**
had a brilliant idea!

He undid his favourite woolly scarf and tied it around the surprised snowman.

Then he replaced the snowman's old black hat with his warm knitted one.

The snowman was so happy! At last he had his very OWN Christmas present!

Oliver and Blitzen flew as fast as they could to get the missing present back in time for **Christmas** morning.

Oliver placed the gift under the tree with a **huge** sigh of relief!

Back at home **Oliver** gave Blitzen a **big hug**, then watched as his new friend flew up into the sky and home to Santa.

When **Oliver** woke up on Christmas morning, he wondered if it had all been a **dream**. Then he looked out of his window...

...and there in the distance was the **happy** snowman waving at him and he was still wearing his **lovely** Christmas present.

The end